SPORTS BIOGRAPHIES

EILEEN GU

KENNY ABDO

Fly!
An Imprint of Abdo Zoom
abdobooks.com

abdobooks.com

Published by Abdo Zoom, a division of ABDO, P.O. Box 398166, Minneapolis, Minnesota 55439. Copyright © 2023 by Abdo Consulting Group, Inc. International copyrights reserved in all countries. No part of this book may be reproduced in any form without written permission from the publisher. Fly!™ is a trademark and logo of Abdo Zoom.

Printed in the United States of America, North Mankato, Minnesota.
102022
012023

Photo Credits: Alamy, AP Images, Getty Images, iStock, Shutterstock
Production Contributors: Kenny Abdo, Jennie Forsberg, Grace Hansen
Design Contributors: Neil Klinepier

Library of Congress Control Number: 2022937312

Publisher's Cataloging-in-Publication Data

Names: Abdo, Kenny, author.
Title: Eileen Gu / by Kenny Abdo
Description: Minneapolis, Minnesota : Abdo Zoom, 2023 | Series: Sports biographies | Includes online resources and index.
Identifiers: ISBN 9781098280246 (lib. bdg.) | ISBN 9781098280772 (ebook) | ISBN 9781098281076 (Read-to-Me ebook)
Subjects: LCSH: Gu, Eileen, 2002---Juvenile literature. | Olympic athletes--Juvenile literature. | Freestyle skiing--Juvenile literature. | Women skiers--Juvenile literature.
Classification: DDC 796.092--dc23

TABLE OF CONTENTS

Eileen Gu 4

Early Years 8

Going Pro 12

Legacy 18

Glossary 22

Online Resources 23

Index 24

EILEEN GU

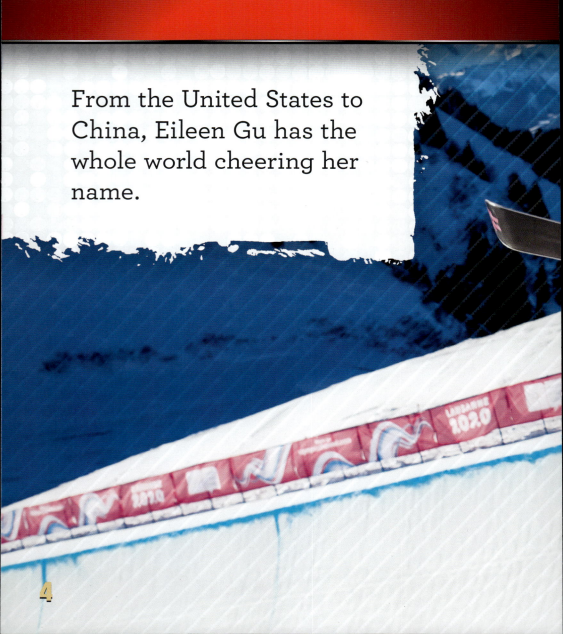

From the United States to China, Eileen Gu has the whole world cheering her name.

The young Olympian earned her spot in the sporting event's history with her win in women's big air. She is among the world's best **freestyle** skiers.

EARLY YEARS

Eileen Feng Gu was born in San Francisco, California, in 2003. Her mother, Yan, **immigrated** from China before Gu was born. Yan raised her daughter as a single parent.

Yan was an **avid** skier. When Eileen was three, her mother began taking her on weekend trips to Tahoe to ski.

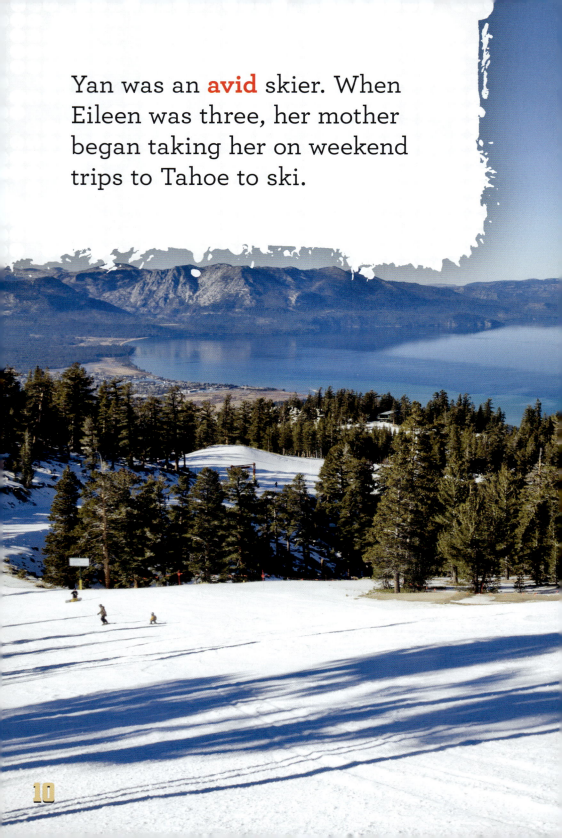

Gu got serious about the sport at eight years old. Her focus was **freestyle**. Gu continued to compete and win many races. Never slowing down with her studies, Gu graduated early from high school.

GOING PRO

In 2018, U.S. head coach of competitive freeskiing, Dave Euler, noticed Gu's talent. He had Gu begin with **slopestyle** skiing. Soon after, Gu was ready for the big leagues.

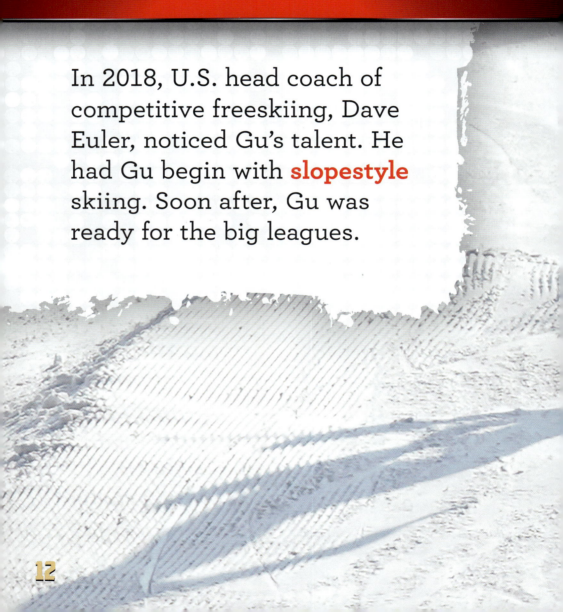

In 2019, while representing the United States, Gu won a World Cup **slopestyle** event in Italy. She was only 15 years old!

Gu announced she would compete for China in 2020. "I am proud of my heritage and equally proud of my American upbringings," she wrote on an Instagram post.

At the 2021 Winter **X Games**, Gu became the first rookie to medal in three events. She was also the first athlete representing China to win a gold medal at the X Games!

Gu wowed the world at the 2022 Winter **Olympics** when she became the first woman to land a leftside **double cork 1620** in a competition. She was also the first **freestyle** skier to win three medals at the winter games.

LEGACY

Gu's influence goes beyond the **slopes**. She supports brands and causes that she believes in. **Social justice** and equality are just some important causes to the Asian American athlete.

With so many medals and records at such a young age, Gu will continue to inspire not only skiing fans, but young girls around the world to reach for the gold.

GLOSSARY

avid – having an eager desire for.

double cork 1620 – a move in which skiers spin four-and-a-half times while rotating twice off-axis.

freestyle – a snow sport that combines acrobatics and skiing and often uses jumps or mounds of snow to perform the tricks in the air.

immigrate – to come to live permanently in a country where one was not born.

Olympic Games – the biggest international athletic event held as separate winter and summer competitions every four years in a different city.

slope – either a snow-covered mountain or man-made structure which you can ski down.

slopestyle – a discipline of freestyle skiing or snowboarding involving an obstacle course.

social justice – the upholding of what is fair, just, and right in terms of wealth, opportunities, and privileges in a society.

X Games – an extreme sports competition that is held twice a year. There is a summer and a winter competition.

ONLINE RESOURCES

To learn more about Eileen Gu, please visit **abdobooklinks.com** or scan this QR code. These links are routinely monitored and updated to provide the most current information available.

California 9

China 4, 9, 15

Euler, Dave 12

family 9, 10

medals 14, 16, 17, 20

Olympics 6, 17

records 17, 20

World Cup 14

X Games 16